First Little Readers™

Ghosterella

by Liza Charlesworth

ISBN: 978-1-338-29796-6

Illustrated by Tammie Lyon

First printing, June 2018.

 Published by Scholastic Inc. Printed in Jiaxing, China.

Once upon a time,
there was a sweet ghost.
Her name was Ghosterella.

She lived in an old house
with three scary sisters.

One day, an invitation came.
The ghost prince was having a ball!

"You can't go!" said the scary sisters. Then off they flew to the ball.

“Boo-hoo!” cried Ghosterella.
A magic bat appeared.
“I will help you go to the ball,”
she said.

The bat flapped her wings.
There was a dress!

The bat flapped her wings again.
There was a watch!

"Be home by 12:00," said the bat.
"I will!" said Ghosterella.
Then off she flew to the ball.

The ball was grand!
Ghosterella met the prince.

They danced and danced.
"I like you," said the prince.
"I like you, too," said Ghosterella.

Ghosterella looked at her watch.
It was almost 12:00.
Oh, no!
She had to go right now!

Ghosterella dropped her watch,
and the prince saw it.
"I will find that ghost girl that
fits this watch," he said.

The prince flew to an old house.
He went inside.
Did the watch fit the scary sisters?
No, no, no!

Did the watch fit Ghosterella?
Yes!
"Will you marry me?" he asked.
"Woo-hoo!" she said.

Ghosterella and the prince had a big, fancy wedding. Then they both flew happily ever after.